MY HENRY

For Tom

First published in hardback in Great Britain by HarperCollins Children's Books in 2011
First published in paperback in 2012

10 9 8 7 6 5 4 3 2 1
ISBN: 978-0-00-738812-7

HarperCollins Children's Books is a division of HarperCollins Publishers Ltd.

A CIP catalogue record for this title is available from the British Library.

Visit our website at: www.harpercollins.co.uk

Printed and bound in China

MY HENRY

Judith Kerr

HarperCollins *Children's Books*

They think I'm sitting in this chair
Just waiting for my tea.

In fact, I'm flying through the air
With Henry holding me.

My Henry died and went to heaven,
But now he's got his wings
They let him out from four till seven
And we do all sorts of things.

In life my Henry was not fond
Of dangerous sports and stunts,

But now he's in the Great Beyond
He does like lion hunts.

It’s things we’ve never tried before
That are the greatest fun,
Like riding on a dinosaur,
Which I had never done.

And sometimes we have jungle feasts
High up among the treetops
With heavenly treats for all the beasts
And self-fulfilling teapots.

They think I'm having forty winks,
But little do they know…

…that I am chatting with the Sphinx
Who's asked us out to Sunday drinks
With several friends in tow.

And as I have no head for heights,
They never can have guessed
That one of our supreme delights
Is climbing Everest.

At night we like to water ski
And greet the sun at dawn.

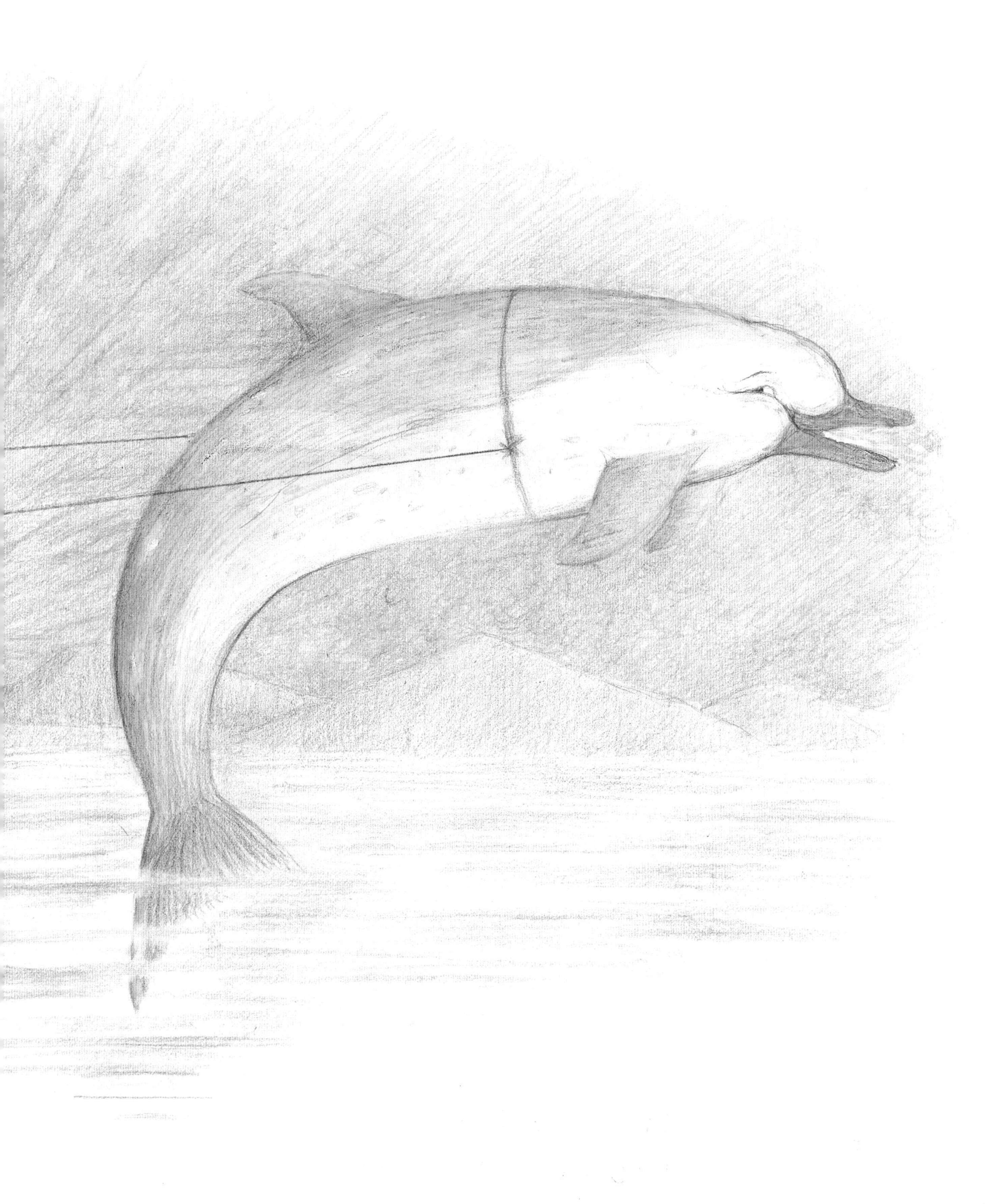

We play with

mermaids in the sea

…and know a unicorn.

But sometimes we prefer to give
The world a miss, because
We picture how we used to live
And think how nice it was.

"See you tomorrow afternoon.
I will be waiting here.
Perhaps we'll picnic on the moon?"

"Two sugars, thank you, dear."

Picture books by Judith Kerr

The Tiger Who Came to Tea*
Mog the Forgetful Cat*
Mog's Christmas*
Mog and the Baby*
Mog in the Dark
Mog's Amazing Birthday Caper
Mog and Bunny
Mog and Barnaby
Mog on Fox Night
Mog and the Granny
Mog and the V.E.T.*
Mog's Bad Thing
Goodbye Mog
When Willy Went to the Wedding
How Mrs Monkey Missed the Ark
Birdie Halleluyah!
The Other Goose
Goose in a Hole
Twinkles, Arthur and Puss*
One Night in the Zoo*

*also available on audio CD